First
Facts ™

Health Matters

Asthma

by Jason Glaser

Consultant:
James R. Hubbard, MD
Fellow in the American Academy of Pediatrics
Iowa Medical Society
West Des Moines, Iowa

Capstone
press

Mankato, Minnesota

First Facts is published by Capstone Press,
151 Good Counsel Drive, P.O. Box 669, Mankato, Minnesota 56002.
www.capstonepress.com

Library of Congress Cataloging-in-Publication Data
Glaser, Jason.
    Asthma / by Jason Glaser.
    p. cm.—(First facts. Health matters)
    Summary: "Describes asthma and its causes, symptoms, and treatments"—Provided
by publisher.
    Includes bibliographical references and index.
    ISBN 0-7368-4287-X (hardcover)
    1. Asthma—Juvenile literature. I. Title. II. Series.
RC591.G56 2006
616.2'38—dc22   2004031021

Editorial Credits
Mari C. Schuh, editor; Juliette Peters, designer; Kelly Garvin, photo researcher/photo editor

Photo Credits
BananaStock, Ltd., 14
Capstone Press/Karon Dubke, cover (foreground), 10, 11, 21
Corbis/Michael Keller, 12–13
Getty Images Inc./John Lund, 20; John Millar, 1
Photo Researchers Inc./Burger, 15, 16; D. Lovegrove, 8–9; Science Photo Library/Jay Coneyl, 6
Rubberball, 19
Visuals Unlimited/Biodisc, cover (background)

1 2 3 4 5 6 10 09 08 07 06 05

Table of Contents

What Is Asthma?

Asthma is an illness in the lungs.
Air going into the lungs moves through
many airways. During an asthma attack,
muscles push some airways closed. A
sticky fluid called **mucus** closes smaller
airways. People with asthma usually
have it for a very long time. Luckily,
asthma attacks can be controlled.

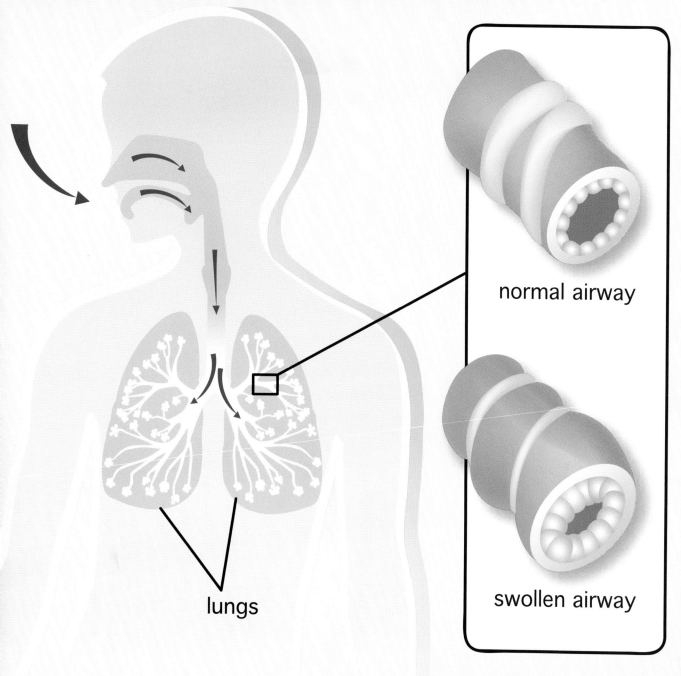

normal airway

swollen airway

lungs

Signs of Asthma

Asthma makes breathing hard. People with asthma feel fine most of the time. But during asthma attacks, people's ribs and chests feel tight. They may **wheeze** and cough. They take short, fast breaths. Breathing out takes much longer.

Fact!
Asthma means "breathing heavy."

How Do Kids Get Asthma?

Doctors aren't always sure why kids get asthma. Kids with **allergies** sometimes have asthma. Small things in the air hurt their lungs.

Doctors know that asthma can run in families. Kids are more likely to have asthma if one of their parents has asthma.

What Else Could It Be?

Not all lung problems are asthma.
Colds and the flu can make people
cough. But the coughing will go away.
Asthma does not go away.

Bronchitis causes swollen airways and coughing. Some people cough up thick mucus. It can be hard to tell the difference between bronchitis and asthma.

Should Kids See a Doctor?

Kids with asthma need to see a doctor. Doctors can help find reasons why asthma attacks start.

Doctors can give people **medicine** to help asthma. The right medicine can prevent asthma attacks.

 Fact!
There is no cure for asthma. With treatment, asthma attacks can go away for many years.

How to Treat Asthma

Many kids with asthma use **inhalers** to breathe in medicine. Kids need to take their medicine at the right time each day.

Kids with asthma should test
their lungs. Each day, they should blow
into a peak flow meter. It measures how
fast they can blow out air.

If It Gets Worse

Colds and the flu can make asthma attacks worse. More mucus makes breathing harder.

Asthma attacks are serious. People who cannot breathe can die. Medicine needs to be taken right away. If medicine doesn't work, the person needs to see a doctor.

Staying Healthy

People with asthma can help themselves stay healthy. Exercising can make lungs stronger. They should stay away from smoke and things that cause allergies. They should also clean often. Cleaning gets rid of germs, bugs, and dust.

! Fact!
One in 13 kids has asthma.

Amazing but True!

According to myth, petting chihuhuas will cure asthma. Parents of kids with asthma sometimes buy these dogs.

Asthma usually gets better as kids get older. Chihuahuas often get breathing problems as they get older. Some people wrongly think the dogs take the asthma away from the kids.

Hands On: Breath Test

Make a breath test to see how much air you can push out of your lungs. Ask an adult to help.

What You Need

2-liter bottle
water
large bowl
marker

2 feet (.6 meter)
of .25-inch
(.6-centimeter)
rubber tubing

What You Do

1. Fill the bottle with water. Fill the bowl half full.
2. Cover the top of the bottle tightly with your hand.
3. Turn the bottle upside down over the bowl.
4. Put your hand and bottle top under the surface of the water.
5. Take your hand away from the bottle top.
6. Have your helper hold the bottle in place.
7. Slide one end of the tube into the bottle.
8. Take a deep breath. Blow hard into the tube.
9. Mark the water level in the bottle with the marker.

Your breath will push air into the bottle. This air pushes water out of the bottle. Try it again to see if your results change.

21

Glossary

allergies (AL-er-jees)—reactions to things like dogs, cats, and dust

inhaler (in-HAY-lur)—a small device used to breathe in medicine through the mouth; inhalers are used to treat asthma.

medicine (MED-uh-suhn)—pills, syrups, and liquids that can make people feel better during an illness

mucus (MYOO-kuhss)—a slimy fluid that coats the inside of your mouth, nose, and throat

wheeze (WEEZ)—to breathe with difficulty, usually making a whistling sound

Read More

Bjorklund, Ruth. *Asthma.* Health Alert. New York: Benchmark Books, 2005.

Royston, Angela. *Asthma.* It's Not Catching. Chicago: Heinemann, 2004.

Silverstein, Alvin, Virginia Silverstein, and Laura Silverstein Nunn. *Asthma.* My Health. New York: Franklin Watts, 2002.

Internet Sites

FactHound offers a safe, fun way to find Internet sites related to this book. All of the sites on FactHound have been researched by our staff.

Here's how:
1. Visit *www.facthound.com*
2. Type in this special code **073684287X** for age-appropriate sites. Or enter a search word related to this book for a more general search.
3. Click on the **Fetch It** button.

FactHound will fetch the best sites for you!

Index